Once there was a girl
a very little girl.
And there was a dragon
a very biggle dragon.

They were friends...

To my cuzzies, Vicki and Donna.
Let's sail to the far-est Far Away!
B. J.

For L. M.
R. C.

First published 2017 by Walker Books Ltd
87 Vauxhall Walk, London SE11 5HJ

2 4 6 8 10 9 7 5 3 1

Text © 2017 Barbara Joosse

Illustrations © 2017 Randy Cecil

The right of Barbara Joosse and Randy Cecil to be identified as author and illustrator respectively of this
work has been asserted by them in accordance with the Copyright, Designs and Patents Act 1988

This book has been typeset in Horley Old Style Semibold

Printed in China

British Library Cataloguing in Publication Data:
a catalogue record for this book is available from the British Library

ISBN 978-1-4063-7693-7

www.walker.co.uk

MIX
Paper from
responsible sources
FSC® C104723

SAIL AWAY DRAGON

Barbara Joosse

illustrated by Randy Cecil

WALKER BOOKS
AND SUBSIDIARIES
LONDON • BOSTON • SYDNEY • AUCKLAND

Forever, Girl lived in the very same castle.

Forever, she slept in the same little bed
  comfy little, pluffy little eiderdown bed.
Same little bed, same little room
very same wish on the very same moon:

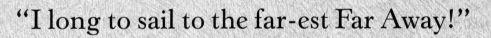

"I long to sail to the far-est Far Away!"

Forever, Dragon lived in the same dragon lair.

Every night was the same as the rest
   a-snoring and a-tossing in his rumble-tumble nest
dreaming, "Big brave ME, sailing from the shore
with GIRL, my friend forevermore."

Sometimes when friends share a heart
they dream the same thing, apart.

And so it was.

Dragon went a little crazy
a little oopsy
doopsy daisy.

"Let's sail away!
Today today!"

Girl packed a wicker basket
such a tisket, such a tasket
with some biscuits
and some honey
and a marshmallow bunny

and a spyglass for to spy with

and a banner to good-bye with

and a box of goodie gumdrops

and a horn.

"All aboard," said Dragon.
"Yo ho," said Girl,
and she waved the good-bye banner
such a flip-flappy banner

and he pounced into the sea

such a lip-lappy sea –

WHEEEEE!

The friends made their way towards the far-est Far Away.

And the dolphins swam beside them

and the sun was there to guide them

and the moon, it came to shine them

evermore evermore on the sea.

Sometimes, there were troubles.

When the breeze died,

Girl blew bubbles.

When Whale spouted – *poof!*

Dragon made a roof.

One dark and snarly night, Bad Hats appeared
in hats with horns and ratty beards.

They rattled their swords and pointed their spears
and shouted, "HEY! Get over here!"

Dragon roared, "NO!
Stay away from Girl, you Bad Hats!"

Bad Hats skedaddled.

And that was that.

Except …

one orange and scrawny cat

jumped upon a wooden raft

and floated close

to snuggle up to Dragon's nose.

For a year and a day, the friends sailed away
searching everywhere for the far-est Far Away:

Up.

 Down.

Around.

They began to despair.

"Will we find the Far Away *anywhere*?"

And then ...

THEY DID!

With Dragon as boat

and Girl as crew

there was nothing – *nothing* – they couldn't do!

Oh, they gulped the goodie gumdrops
and they danced the jerry jig

and they blew the
merry horn
and they wrote the
very note

and they launched it
in a bottle from the boat:
"Girl and Dragon were here!"

That night, Girl curled

beneath Dragon's wing

both of them dreaming the very same thing:

Home.

And they sailed home for a year and a day,
finding surprises along the way –

a shark with no teeth

an orange coral reef

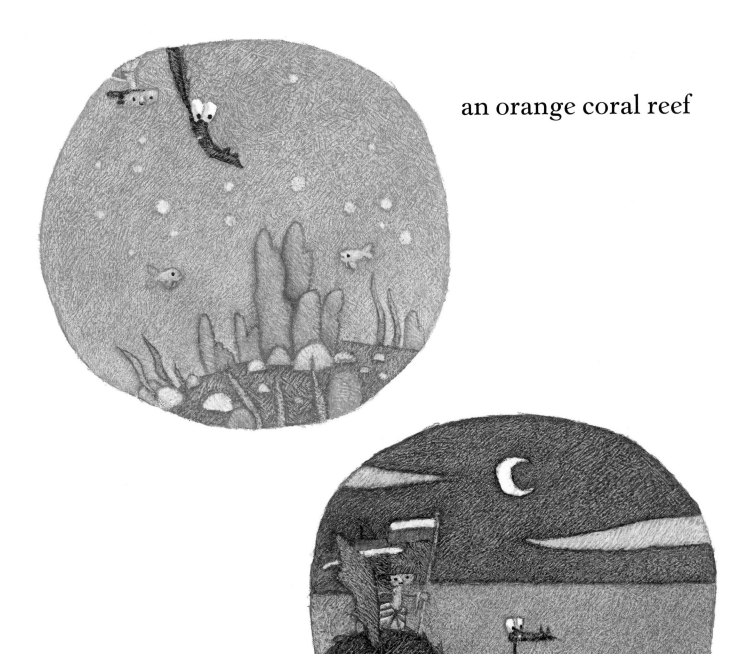

and an owl

strumming tunes

to the man in the moon.

Then they were Home. Ahh.

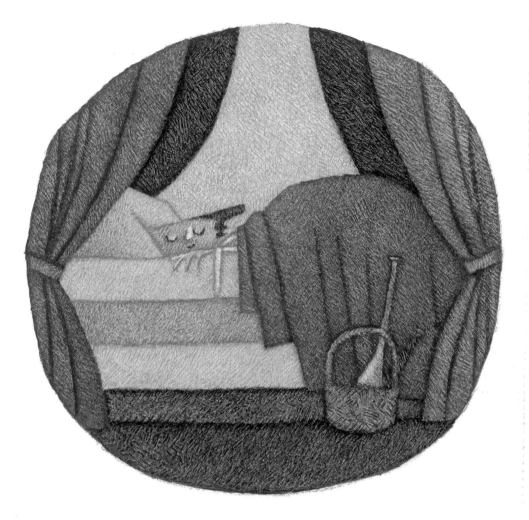

Girl, fast asleep in her very own bed

comfy little, pluffy little eiderdown bed.

Now Dragon, curled above the castle door,
guarding Girl, his friend forevermore.

Home.